CHECKERBOARD BIOGRAPHIES

MICHAEL JORDAN

REBECCA FELIX

Checkerboard Library

An Imprint of Abdo Publishing
abdobooks.com

ABDOBOOKS.COM

Published by Abdo Publishing, a division of ABDO, PO Box 398166, Minneapolis, Minnesota 55439.
Copyright © 2022 by Abdo Consulting Group, Inc. International copyrights reserved in all countries.
No part of this book may be reproduced in any form without written permission from the publisher.
Checkerboard Library™ is a trademark and logo of Abdo Publishing.

Printed in the United States of America, North Mankato, Minnesota
052021
092021

 THIS BOOK CONTAINS
RECYCLED MATERIALS

Design and Production: Mighty Media, Inc.
Editor: Liz Salzmann
Cover Photograph: Tom DiPace/AP Images
Interior Photographs: AlxMendezR/Shutterstock Images, pp. 19, 28 (bottom right); AP Images, pp. 9, 28;
    CHARLES BENNETT/AP Images, p. 15; Dave Martin/AP Images, p. 17; FRANK POLICH/AP Images, pp. 21,
    29 (bottom); FRED JEWELL/AP Images, p. 5; JACK SMITH/AP Images, p. 13; JOHN SWART/AP Images,
    p. 11; landmarkmedia/Shutterstock Images, pp. 23, 28 (bottom left); Office of the President/Wikimedia
    Commons, p. 27; Seth Poppel/Yearbook Library, p. 7; Shutterstock Images, p. 23 (paper clip); Zach
    Catanzareti Photo/Flickr, pp. 25, 29

Library of Congress Control Number: 2021932874

Publisher's Cataloging-in-Publication Data
Names: Felix, Rebecca, author.
Title: Michael Jordan / by Rebecca Felix
Description: Minneapolis, Minnesota : Abdo Publishing, 2022 | Series: Checkerboard biographies | Includes
    online resources and index.
Identifiers: ISBN 9781532196010 (lib. bdg.) | ISBN 9781098216870 (ebook)
Subjects: LCSH: Jordan, Michael, 1963- --Juvenile literature. | Basketball players--United States--
    Biography--Juvenile literature. | African American basketball players--Biography--Juvenile literature. |
    Guards (Basketball)--Biography--Juvenile literature. | Professional athletes--United States--Biography--
    Juvenile literature. | Chicago Bulls (Basketball team)--Juvenile literature.
Classification: DDC 796.323092--dc23

CONTENTS

CHAPTER 1

HIS AIRNESS

Many people consider Michael Jordan the greatest basketball player of all time. He played 15 seasons in the National Basketball Association (NBA). During that time, he won many awards, titles, and honors. But it is an award from ESPN that truly captures Jordan's achievements. The sports channel named him North American Athlete of the Century.

Jordan's talent and appeal changed the entire sport of basketball. His influence expanded beyond the court. He affected several generations of athletes across multiple sports.

Jordan's nicknames "Air Jordan" and "His Airness" refer to his impressive vertical leap when scoring slam dunks. But soaring to great heights doesn't only describe Jordan's physical feats. He is famous for having high expectations of himself and others. From a young age, Jordan was focused on becoming great.

 You must expect great things of yourself before you can do them.

Jordan played in the NBA All-Star Game 13 times.

CHAPTER 2

ATHLETIC UPBRINGING

Michael Jeffrey Jordan was born on February 17, 1963, in Brooklyn, New York. His parents were James and Deloris. Michael had two brothers and two sisters. They were Larry, James Jr., Roslyn, and Deloris.

When Michael was young, his family moved to Wilmington, North Carolina. Sports were a big part of Michael's childhood, especially baseball and basketball. His father even built a basketball court in the family's backyard.

Michael played on the **varsity** basketball team at Emsley A. Laney High School. In 1981, as a senior, he earned a basketball **scholarship** to attend the University of North Carolina. There, he would play basketball and study **cultural** geography.

CLOSE CALL

Michael attended baseball camp as a boy and nearly drowned during a swimming activity. Ever since, he has had a fear of large bodies of water.

Michael started wearing number 23 on his high school varsity team.

CHAPTER 3

COLLEGE & PRO ATHLETE

Jordan's first year of college basketball ended in a memorable victory. In the 1982 National Collegiate Athletic Association (NCAA) championship game, Jordan scored 16 points. This included the game-winning basket with less than 20 seconds left in the game!

The next year, the *Sporting News* named Jordan the College Player of the Year. In June 1984, Jordan was **drafted** by the Chicago Bulls. He decided to leave college after his junior year. He wanted to focus on his professional basketball career.

The same summer, Jordan was chosen to be on the US Olympic basketball team. The 1984 Summer Olympic Games were held in Los Angeles, California. Jordan helped the United States win the gold medal.

That fall, Jordan's first season with the Bulls started. With Jordan on the team, the Bulls won 11 more games than in the previous season. When the season ended in May 1985, the NBA named Jordan Rookie of the Year.

In the 1984 Olympics, Jordan averaged 17.1 points per game. This was the most of any player on the US team.

CHAPTER 4

AIR JORDAN

In October 1984, Jordan had signed a deal with Nike. He would represent the sports brand in ads and by wearing Nike shoes and clothing. Jordan also worked with Nike to design the items made for him.

In 1985, Nike released a shoe in honor of Jordan. Air Jordan 1 shoes were named after Jordan's reputation for jumping high in the air to dunk balls. It also referred to the way the shoes would cushion the wearer's feet. Jordan received 25 percent of the shoe's sales. This would make Jordan incredibly wealthy, as Air Jordans became one of history's most successful shoe brands.

From early in Jordan's career, fans and fellow players copied both his style of playing and his fashion. When he joined the NBA, players' shorts were fairly short and tight. But Jordan wanted to wear his old college basketball shorts under his Bulls uniform, for luck. To keep the college shorts hidden, he wore longer, baggier Bulls shorts. As Jordan's fame rose, other players

Scottie Pippen (*right*) joined the Bulls in 1987. He and Jordan (*left*) were two of the team's star players.

adopted this look. This style of shorts became standard among most basketball players around the world.

Jordan began winning awards early in his career. In the 1987–1988 season, he was named the NBA's Most Valuable Player (MVP). He also earned the season's scoring title and was named the Defensive Player of the Year. This made Jordan the first player in history to achieve both in the same season.

In September 1989, Jordan took on the title of husband when he married Juanita Vanoy. The couple had three children, Jeffrey, Marcus, and Jasmine. Jordan and Vanoy's marriage lasted 17 years.

In spring 1991, the Bulls made it to the NBA Finals. Jordan had been a key player in helping the Bulls get there. He also helped win the championship! It was the Bulls' first NBA title. Jordan also won the NBA's scoring title that season.

Winning the championship and the scoring title was a historic feat. Jordan was the fourth NBA player ever to win both in the same season. He repeated this five times in his career. As of 2021, he remained the only NBA player to achieve both in the same season more than once.

Jordan (*left*) and Bulls head coach Phil Jackson (*right*) celebrate after winning the 1998 NBA title. Jackson was head coach from 1989 to 1998. During that time, the team won six NBA titles.

CHAPTER 5

WINS, LOSSES & BASEBALL

In spring 1992, Jordan completed his usual outstanding NBA season. That summer, Jordan played on the US Olympic team. It was called the "Dream Team" because it included the best American players. The team traveled to Barcelona, Spain, for the 1992 Summer Olympics. By this time, Jordan had fans around the world. They watched him help the Dream Team win gold.

This win was followed by another successful season in the NBA. Jordan and the Bulls won the NBA title for the third straight year. Jordan was named the 1993 Finals MVP, also for the third year in a row.

Shortly after these wins, Jordan suffered a great loss. In July 1993, his father died. Jordan thought about the last conversation he had with his father. Jordan had said he was interested in switching from basketball to baseball. Baseball was a shared loved between him and his father. James encouraged his son's idea.

Jordan celebrating his twenty-sixth birthday with his mother and father. The cake is shaped like an Air Jordan shoe.

On October 6, 1993, Jordan announced that he was retiring from basketball. Then in February 1994, he announced he had signed with the Chicago White Sox, a Major League Baseball (MLB) team.

Jordan was one of basketball's most talented stars. But in baseball, he had to prove himself. The White Sox assigned Jordan to one of its minor league teams, the Birmingham Barons of Alabama. Attendance at Barons games rose with Jordan on the team.

Over the summer and winter, Jordan worked hard on improving his baseball skills. But by spring 1995, MLB players were on **strike**. To join MLB spring training, players would have to cross the **picket line**. Jordan and many other minor league players refused to do this, to support the MLB players.

Jordan decided to return to basketball rather than wait for the MLB strike to end. In March 1995, the Bulls announced Jordan would rejoin the team. Jordan's press release had just two words. It said, "I'm back."

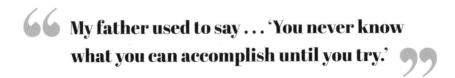

My father used to say . . . 'You never know what you can accomplish until you try.'

Jordan played left field with the Barons. During his time on the team, he hit three home runs.

CHAPTER 6

RETURN & RETIREMENT

Jordan's return to the NBA was celebrated by the league, his teammates, and fans everywhere. During the years without Jordan, the Bulls had lost its championship winning streak. With Jordan back on the team, the Bulls once again won the NBA title in 1996. Jordan was named the NBA Finals MVP. And he once again led the league in points.

In July 1996, Jordan signed a one-year, $30 million contract with the Bulls. This was the largest amount any athlete in history had been paid for a single season. Three months later, Jordan made the NBA's list of the 50 Greatest Players in NBA History.

On November 15, Jordan revealed a new skill. He made his acting **debut** in the movie *Space Jam*. The film includes both live action and **animation**. Jordan starred as himself, playing basketball with a cast of Looney Tunes cartoon characters. Critics gave the film mixed reviews,

In 1994, the Bulls honored Jordan with a statue at its home arena, the United Center. The statue shows Jordan in midair, about to dunk a ball.

but it was very successful at the box office. *Space Jam* earned $230 million in ticket sales!

In 1997 and 1998, Jordan led the Bulls to win two more championships. And each time, the NBA again named him the NBA Finals MVP. Jordan's June 14, 1998, performance in Game 6 of the finals became legendary.

The Bulls had just scored to tie the game against the Utah Jazz. Jordan had the ball with 20 seconds left in the game. Jazz player Bryon Russell was guarding him. Jordan dribbled to the right and pulled a crossover move, evading Russell. Jordan jumped, shot, and *swoosh*! The winning basket!

Jordan pumped his hands in the air, holding up six fingers. He had just won his team's sixth NBA title. That basket would be Jordan's last for the Bulls.

The 1998–1999 NBA season was delayed due to a **lockout**. It still hadn't started in January 1999, when Jordan announced his second retirement from basketball. He told the media he was 99.9 percent sure he wouldn't return. Many people saw this as the end of an era for the beloved star, the Bulls, and the entire NBA.

Jordan received his fifth league MVP award in 1998.

CHAPTER 7

CULTURAL IMPACT

Eleven months after Jordan's retirement, ESPN named him North American Athlete of the Century. Though Jordan was no longer on the basketball court, he had forever changed the sport. Jordan is credited with the **globalization** of basketball. A **silhouette** of him in a vertical leap, basketball in hand, became a global symbol for the sport, and for athletic achievement.

Incredible natural skill was just one part of Jordan's excellence. His **work ethic** was also extraordinary. Teammates said Jordan put as much effort into training as he did into playing during games. Jordan wanted to win. And he pushed others to rise to his level. This attitude and **dedication** shaped the way future generations approached the game.

But Jordan's influence went beyond basketball. He became an idol across all sports. Historians say he redefined what it meant to be a successful athlete. Jordan's rise to fame and his time with the Bulls is considered legendary. And even after retirement, his star continued to blaze.

BIO BASICS

NAME: Michael Jeffrey Jordan

NICKNAMES: Air Jordan,
His Airness

BIRTH: February 17, 1963, Brooklyn, New York

SPOUSES: Juanita Vanoy (1989-2006), Yvette
Prieto (2013-present)

CHILDREN: Jeffrey, Marcus, Jasmine,
Victoria, Ysabel

FAMOUS FOR: jumping very high to slam
dunk the basketball, scoring many points
per game, Air Jordan shoes

ACHIEVEMENTS: NBA Rookie of the Year, six
NBA championships, five NBA MVP awards, on
the NBA's list of the 50 Greatest Players
in NBA History, two Olympic gold medals,
named North American Athlete of the
Century by ESPN

CHAPTER 8

POST RETIREMENT

After his retirement, Jordan focused on many different businesses. He continued to work with Nike on its Jordan brand. And in 1998, he opened restaurants in several US states.

Then in 2000, Jordan returned to the NBA. This time, he was part owner of the Washington Wizards. But by September 2001, Jordan decided he wanted to play again. He sold his ownership of the Wizards and signed a two-year contract to play for the team. Jordan had two successful seasons. He retired for good after the 2002–2003 season. In 2006, he became part owner of the Charlotte Hornets in North Carolina.

Meanwhile, Jordan pursued an interest in racing. In 2004, he started motorcycle team Michael Jordan Motorsports. In fall 2020, Jordan and race car driver Denny Hamlin established the NASCAR team 23XI Racing.

EXPANDING FAMILY

In 2007, Jordan met Yvette Prieto. The two began dating and married in 2013. In 2014, Prieto gave birth to her and Jordan's twin daughters, Victoria and Ysabel.

The first race 23XI Racing competed in was the Daytona 500 in February 2021. Bubba Wallace drove the car in the race and finished seventeenth.

CHAPTER 9

ETERNAL ICON

Jordan made history countless times during his career. When he finally retired, he had scored a total of 32,292 points. This made his average 30.12 points per game, the best in NBA history.

Jordan's off-court ventures were equally incredible. In 2008, Jordan was named the Chief Wish Ambassador for the Make-A-Wish Foundation. The organization grants the wishes of children with serious illnesses. In 2009, Jordan was **inducted** into the Naismith Memorial Basketball Hall of Fame.

Historians, the media, and fans continue to reflect on Jordan's **cultural** influence. In 2020, ESPN aired *The Last Dance*. This ten-part **documentary** series gave an in-depth look at Jordan's prime NBA years.

The series' content **confirmed** Jordan's amazing effect on the league, the game, and his teammates. And the creation and success of the series itself proved his lasting appeal as a cultural icon. Nearly four decades after his NBA **debut**, Michael Jordan remains a global symbol of athletic greatness and inspiration.

In 2016, President Barack Obama (*right*) gave Jordan the Presidential Medal of Freedom for his contributions to US culture.

TIMELINE

1963
Michael Jeffrey Jordan is born on February 17 in Brooklyn, New York.

1984
Jordan is drafted by the Chicago Bulls. He wins a gold medal as part of the US Olympic basketball team.

1992
Jordan wins a second Olympic gold medal, as part of the Dream Team.

1994
Jordan joins the White Sox's minor league team, the Birmingham Barons.

1981
Michael receives a basketball scholarship from the University of North Carolina.

1991
Jordan helps the Bulls win its first NBA title.

1993
Jordan announces his retirement from basketball.

1996

Jordan is named to the list of the 50 Greatest Players in NBA History. He appears in the movie *Space Jam*.

2001

Jordan returns to basketball, playing for the Washington Wizards.

2003

Jordan retires from playing basketball for the last time.

2020

Jordan and Denny Hamlin form NASCAR team 23XI Racing.

1995

Jordan quits baseball and returns to the Bulls.

1999

Jordan retires from basketball for the second time. ESPN names him North American Athlete of the Century.

CHICAGO BULLS

GLOSSARY

animation—a process involving a projected series of drawings that appear to move due to slight changes in each drawing.

confirm—to definitively state or prove true something that was previously uncertain.

cultural—of or relating to the customs, arts, and tools of a nation or a people at a certain time.

debut—a first appearance.

dedication—a commitment to a goal or a way of life.

documentary—a film that artistically presents facts, often about an event or a person.

draft—a system for or act of selecting individuals from a group. People may be drafted for required military service or sports teams.

globalization—the act or process of making something known or popular around the world.

induct—to admit as a member.

lockout—when an employer tries to make workers accept certain conditions by refusing to let them come to work until those conditions are accepted.

picket line—a group of people who are refusing to go to work until their employer agrees to certain demands.

scholarship—money or aid given to help a student continue his or her studies.

silhouette (sih-luh-WEHT)—a dark outline seen against a lighter background.

strike—a period of time when workers stop work in order to force an employer to agree to their demands.

varsity—the main team that represents a school in athletic or other competition.

work ethic—a belief in the benefit and importance of work and its ability to strengthen a person's character.

ONLINE RESOURCES

Booklinks
NONFICTION NETWORK
FREE! ONLINE NONFICTION RESOURCES

To learn more about Michael Jordan, please visit **abdobooklinks.com** or scan this QR code. These links are routinely monitored and updated to provide the most current information available.

INDEX